# A TIGER CALLED THOMAS

Story by

## CHARLOTTE ZOLOTOW

Pictures by

## DIANA CAIN BLUTHENTHAL

HYPERION BOOKS FOR CHILDREN

NEW YORK

Text copyright © 1963 by Charlotte Zolotow
Illustrations copyright © 2003 by Diana Cain Bluthenthal

For information address Hyperion Books for Children, 114 Fifth Avenue, New York, New York, 10011-5690.
Printed in Singapore
The artwork was created with a variety of watercolors, acrylics, black ink and collage.
This book is set in 18-point Oneleigh.
Library of Congress Cataloging-in-Publication Data
Zolotow, Charlotte, 1915–
A tiger called Thomas / Charlotte Zolotow; illustrations by Diana Cain Bluthenthal.
p.    cm.
Summary: Thomas realizes being the new kid on the block isn't too lonely
after a special night of trick-or-treating.
ISBN 0-7868-0517-X    [1. Moving, Household—Fiction. 2. Friendship—Fiction.
3. Halloween—Fiction.]
I. Bluthenthal, Diana Cain, ill.  PZ7.Z77 Ti  2003  [E]—dc21  2001051851

Visit www.hyperionchildrensbooks.com

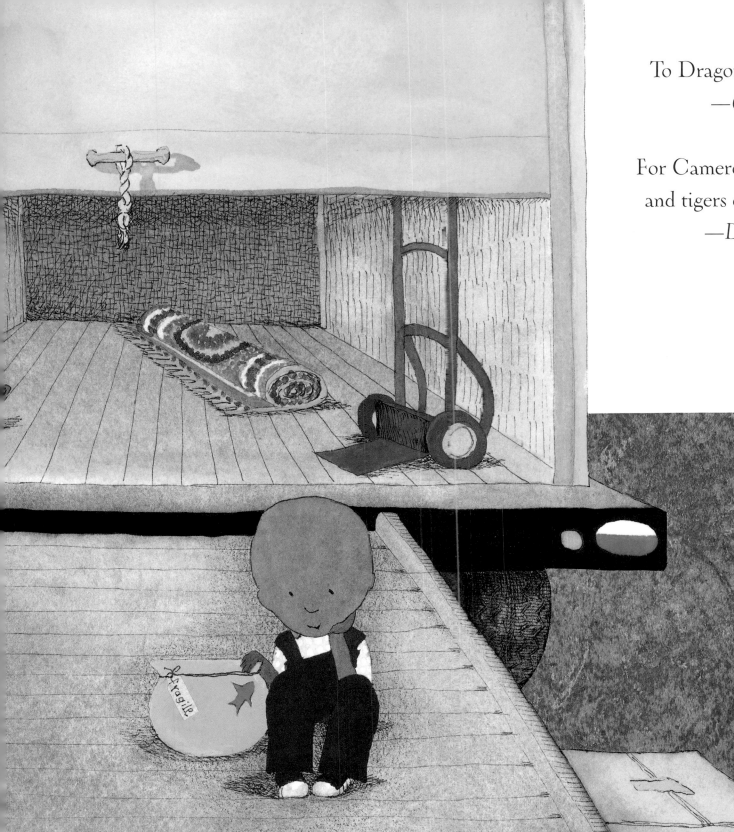

To Dragon and Zee
—CZ

For Cameron & Kelley
and tigers everywhere
—DCB

Once there was a little boy named Thomas.
He was very nice.

But when he and his family moved to a new house on a new street,
he took it into his head that the new people might not like him.

So he never left his stoop.

"Why don't you play with that little girl, Marie?" his mother asked him.

"Maybe she wouldn't like me," Thomas said.

"Of course she'd like you," his mother said. "Why wouldn't she?"

But Thomas didn't answer.

"Why don't you visit the lady
with the black cat down the
street?" his mother asked.

"They might not like me,"
Thomas said.

"Of course they'd like you.
Why shouldn't they like you?"
said his mother.

But Thomas didn't go.

"That tall boy named Gerald looks lonely," his mother said.
"I don't think he'd like me," said Thomas.
"Of course he'd like you," said Thomas's mother.
"Why shouldn't he like you? Everybody likes you."
But Thomas wouldn't leave his stoop.

He just sat there and watched
when Marie played hopscotch.

He sat there and watched
the old woman's cat as it prowled
through the grass and shrubs.

He sat there and watched when
Gerald walked past the house, and
thought how tall he was.

"Oh, Thomas," said his mother. "Everyone will like you.
Why don't you go play?"
But Thomas shook his head and just sat on the steps . . . watching.

The lady in the house across the street was always
out in her yard, watering the plants, raking the leaves,
sweeping the walk, picking her flowers.

And all the while, Thomas sat on his stoop and watched.

He watched the old man who came up the street with his big black poodle three times a day. The poodle always looked over its shoulder at Thomas, and its tail stood up like a small palm tree and wagged from side to side.

But Thomas just sat on his steps and watched them pass.

He watched the sparrows and the grackles and the blue jays in the trees.
He watched the black cat look up at the sparrows and grackles and blue jays.
But he never went off the stoop to play.

At Halloween his mother came home with a tiger costume for him.
"Try this on," she said.

Thomas put on the orange-and-black-striped suit with its quilted tail.

He put on the mask, with its long whiskers.

"How do I look?" he asked his mother.

"Exactly like a tiger," she said.

Thomas looked in the mirror, and his mother was right.

"No one will know who I am when I go trick-or-treating," he said.

There was a large orange moon in the sky, and it was already getting dark when Thomas went out. The branches of the trees hardly showed, except where they laced across the moon.

He crossed the street to the house of the lady who was always outside. The chrysanthemums were still blooming in front of her house.

"Trick or treat," Thomas called when she came to the door.
"Well, hello!" the lady said. She dropped a package of
orange candies into his bag. "Happy Halloween."

"Thank you," answered the tiger.
"You're welcome, Thomas," the lady said, closing the door.
Under his mask, Thomas flushed.
"That's funny," he said to himself. "She called the tiger Thomas."

At the next house he rang the bell.
"Trick or treat," he called.

Marie's mother opened the door. She had candy apples for the treat.

"Oh, thank you," the tiger said, for he especially liked candy apples.

"You're welcome," said Marie's mother. "Marie is a witch tonight.

Maybe you'll pass her, but anyway, come play hopscotch here tomorrow,

Thomas."

"Thank you," Thomas said again. But when the door closed,
he reached up to feel his mask. It was still on, covering his whole face.
That's funny, he thought. She knew who I was, too.

He passed a tall ghost going up to the house as he left.

He couldn't see the ghost's face, but there was something very familiar about this figure.

"Hi, Thomas," said the ghost. "Want to play horseshoes tomorrow? I got a new set."

"Sure," said Thomas. For the ghost was Gerald. Thomas could tell by the height.

He went to the old man's house.

The black poodle threw back his head and barked wildly when he saw the tiger at the door. But when he sniffed at the tiger's feet and sniffed at the tiger's quilted tail, he suddenly put up his own palm-tree tail and wagged it hard.

"Trick or treat," the tiger said.

The old man had made big pumpkin cookies. "Fresh baked, Thomas," he said, winking as he dropped one in the bag.

"Best thing for tigers," he added, and winked again as he watched the tiger go down the steps.

He called the tiger Thomas, too, thought Thomas.

Now he rang the bell at the house of the old lady and the black cat.

"Trick or treat," he called.

"Come in, come in," the little old woman said. Her black cat looked curiously at the tiger, and the tiger reached out to stroke the cat's black, slippery fur.

"He loves that." The little old lady laughed. "Come play with him again, Thomas," she said. "He gets lonely."

"So do I," said Thomas.

She knew, too, he thought to himself as he turned toward home.

The orange moon was a little higher in the sky. The sky was a little blacker than before. He couldn't see any of the branches against it, now.

A group of ghosts and goblins was coming down the steps of the lady across the street. And a solitary but familiar-looking witch with her broom under her arm passed him. He looked at her curiously as he walked slowly toward the steps of his house. It was Marie.

"Hi, Thomas," called Marie.

Thomas walked upstairs to his own room. He looked in the mirror at the tiger. The tiger in the mirror looked back at him, whiskers and all.

"Have a good time?" asked his mother.

"How did they know who I am?" Thomas asked.

"Did they?" said his mother.

"Yes," Thomas said. "The mask didn't fool them a bit.
And they all asked me to come back."

"I guess they all like you," his mother said.

Thomas looked at her. Suddenly he felt wonderful.

"Oh, I like them, too!" he said.
And when he took off the mask, he was smiling.